Courage on the Causeway

by Sarah B. Beurskens

Cover Illustration: Dea Marks
Inside Illustration: Dea Marks

To Dad, who has taught me quiet courage, and to Mom for remaining faithful throughout the journey

Special thanks to Karen Vail, naturalist and nature lover, for checking the facts of this book and for being an enthusiastic teacher of the environment.

About the Author

Sarah Beurskens lives in a remote mountain town called Steamboat Springs, Colorado.

Along with her husband Mike and two sons, Charlie and Will, she likes to explore the creeks and mountains around their home. The Devil's Causeway, on which this story is based, is located about 40 miles south of Steamboat Springs.

© 2001 Perfection Learning®
First ebook edition 2012
www.perfectionlearning.com

10 11 12 13 14 QG 17 16 15 14 13 12

58539
PB ISBN: 978-0-7891-5110-0
RLB ISBN: 978-0-7807-9053-7
eISBN: 978-1-6138-4933-0

Printed in the United States of America

Contents

1. Troubled on the Trail 5

2. The Devil's Causeway 11

3. Brush with the Enemy 19

4. Trapped in the White Wasteland . . . 22

5. A Cry for Help 29

6. To the Rescue?! 36

7. No Way Out 42

8. Rain, Wind, and Fear 46

9. Focus on the Plan 52

10. A Good Different 59

1

Troubled on the Trail

"What do you call *that*?" Amanda asked cruelly.

"It's a—a sh—shawl," Gabby responded. She wrapped the shawl around her shoulders more tightly.

"It looks like something my grandmother would wear," Amanda's friend Jennifer said. Jennifer wrinkled her nose and rolled her eyes.

Amanda and Jennifer walked off, laughing at Gabby. They left her alone in the girls' restroom.

Gabby remembered that moment from last year. Now it was July. Gabby was on a trail in the middle of the Rocky Mountains. She had run into Amanda at the grocery store that morning. That had stirred up the bad memories.

She kicked a rock in the middle of the path. Green aspen leaves fluttered in the wind. They hate me, she thought.

Gabby picked up her pace. She almost bumped into a fallen pine tree blocking the trail. She climbed up onto it.

Gabby sighed. I know why they hate me, she reflected. It's because I'm so dumb.

I can't read. I can't write. I'm 14 years old, and I can't even read a page in a stupid book! Gabby's thoughts raced through her head.

She remembered the first day of school last year. It had been her first day at a new school. Her family had just moved to Colorado.

"Gabby," said Mrs. Wright. "Could you please read the next section?"

"The N—Nazi . . ." Gabby blinked her eyes. Chunks of letters stared up at her. None of them made any sense.

"Nazi," piped in Amanda, pronouncing the word correctly.

"Nazi P—Pa—arty had t—t—taking . . ."

"Taken," barked Amanda again.

"T—taken," Gabby repeated. The letters continued to glare at her.

"You mean you can't even *read*? I can't believe it!" Jennifer said loudly. She looked at Gabby with a stunned expression.

"That will be enough, Jennifer," Mrs. White scolded. "Thank you for trying, Gabriella. John, would you continue?"

Jennifer and Amanda stared at Gabby. Other kids also looked at her. Tears burned at the corners of her eyes.

The thought of that moment brought tears again. Gabby wished her family had never moved here. But just as the words jumped into her mind, she was sorry for thinking them.

It wasn't true. In the beginning, she'd been thrilled to come. Every summer for the past five years, her family had come here from Los Angeles. It had been a long trip by bus.

They came to be with her grandfather. He was a sheepherder in the Rocky Mountains.

It was always so much fun. She enjoyed an escape from the smog of the city, the tall buildings, the crowded streets, and the dirty sidewalks.

In Colorado everything seemed brand-new. Everything looked so clean. It was like the snow washed away the stains every winter. A pretty, new landscape appeared for spring and summer.

She'd been so excited when her mother said they were finally moving out here. The mountains set her free. She loved living near them. But she didn't know exactly what drew her to them.

When she was in school, she sat and looked out the window. She daydreamed she was in the mountains. In her classroom at her desk, she felt like a prisoner. But here among the tall evergreens, the white aspen trees, and the grassy meadows, Gabby felt true freedom.

Sometimes she had to help her grandfather with the sheep. She didn't mind helping him. In fact, it was fun.

Her favorite part was when they moved the sheep to a different grazing spot. They'd run them right down the middle of the highway. All the cars and trucks would have to stop. Every driver had to wait until the sheep passed.

The smiling people inside the cars would watch the moving sheep. Little children with wide eyes would point at Gabby. Then they'd point to the sheep. It was such an adventure.

Gabby smiled and wiped her eyes. Why can't I just stay out here in the woods? she thought. Why do I have to go to school? Even though it was July, Gabby already dreaded the thought of going back to school.

"Grandfather could teach me here," Gabby spoke aloud. He had taught her a lot already.

"*Gabriella, my love, you are a strong girl. Be strong. If you ever get into trouble in these mountains,*" he would speak softly in Spanish, "*the first thing to remember is to stay calm. Then you will think of an answer. You can do anything you set your mind to. But remember, stay calm.*"

Gabby looked around at the tall evergreens and aspens. She felt safe. She couldn't imagine getting in trouble here.

Suddenly a sharp pain shot through her right hand. She looked down. Blood oozed from two fingertips.

Gabby looked back. A tall thistle was on the side of the trail. She must have hit it with her hand as she walked by.

Gabby wiped her throbbing fingers on her jeans. She ignored the pain and continued walking on the trail. She wanted to make it to the base of the causeway before lunchtime.

2

The Devil's Causeway

Birds were chirping. The sun was shining. Tufts of white clouds danced in the sky. The mountains were glorious. They were full of green and dotted with colorful wildflowers. Gabby had never seen the flowers look so pretty!

Ahead, a stream flowed across the trail. The path was muddy where the water crossed it. Gabby hopped from one stone to the next to avoid the mud.

The tracks in the mud caught her eye. She knelt down to study them. Several U-shaped prints clearly marked the path of horses. Outfitters must be on the trail, Gabby thought.

The smaller prints looked like dog paws. There were many small prints that looked like tire treads. Those were hiking boots. One boot looked as if it was about her size.

She didn't find any wild-animal prints on the trail. The animals were smarter than to be where the people were. She'd see wild-animal prints later when she got up in the hills.

She loved seeing all the different animal tracks. Often she would draw the prints for her grandfather. Then he would tell her what animal they belonged to. He knew every animal's track.

Sometimes Gabby and her grandfather would camp out. Grandfather knew so much about the outdoors.

At night, he would build a campfire. Then he would tell her tales of the animals in the forest. Her favorite was the one about the marmots.

"Every night around dusk," her grandfather would say in his soothing Spanish, "all the marmots come out and greet each other—mommas, daddies, and babies.

They jump up on rocks and whistle, calling one another. Others whistle back. It's like they're having a party."

Gabby imagined how fun it would be to have a marmot party. She'd seen marmots up on the mountainside. She gave them names. Jorge was the fat marmot.

She named another one Maria. That one she named after her older sister. Her older sister hadn't liked that idea.

Gabby's thoughts of marmot parties made her feel better. She began to pick up her pace on the path. She loved these mountains—especially in the middle of July.

The wildflowers were amazing. Indian paintbrushes greeted her with spikes of red and hot pink.

Purple lupines pointed to heaven. Gabby knew she couldn't touch the lupines because they were poisonous. Many people saw their fuzzy pea pods and said, "Oh, peas, let's eat them." Her grandfather had told her of people he knew who had gotten sick because of this.

She rounded a bend in the trail. Scampering off the path, Gabby sliced through tall grass over to a group of trees. Gabby stopped at a twisted aspen tree. She reached for her walking stick.

Gabby had found the stick on an earlier hike. It was white and smooth. It bent in a right angle at the top. The bend was perfect for a handrest.

Gabby kept the walking stick hidden by the trees. If she took it home, she knew her sister or brother would take it.

Then Gabby rejoined the trail. Yellow sunflowers strained their thin necks toward the sun.

She passed false forget-me-nots, Jacob's ladders, and huckleberries. Oh, how she loved to eat the huckleberries! Her grandfather picked them for her.

There was a saying about berries in the woods. "Red or white, don't take a bite unless you know what it is."

But the lesson had come a little too late. Gabby had become very ill once when she ate something she thought was a huckleberry but wasn't. She didn't want to risk that again.

Beyond the huckleberries was a fork in the path. To the left, the trail followed the lake and its source. This wasn't the one Gabby chose.

She wanted to climb high—to be on top of the world. She chose the path that would take her above the trees.

Blue chiming bells announced water up ahead. Gabby knew the bell-shaped flowers only grew along streams or other wet areas.

Sure enough, when she turned the corner, a babbling brook was gurgling down the mountain. It skipped over the rocks and branches. The water glistened in the partly shadowed sun.

Gabby sat down on a log that had fallen over the brook. She reached into her jacket pocket and pulled out a tortilla and some cheese. Her mother had made the tortilla.

Although she'd eaten this many times at home, it seemed to taste better here in the fresh mountain air. She saved her peach and nuts for later.

Gabby finished her snack and hopped off the log. She continued on the trail. The area was steep with aspen trees and boulders on one side. It sloped down to the lake on the other side. The trail cut flatly across the slope. From here she had an open view of the whole south side.

Gabby paused. She was no longer looking toward the trail. Her eyes followed the mass of rock in front of her. The lake shimmered with the mirror images of the mountains.

These mountains did not come to peaks like others she'd seen in Colorado and California. Each of these mountains came up to a point and flattened into a table. They were called *mesas*, the Spanish word for "tables." Gabby was proud that they had a Spanish name.

To the left, she could see a black mass that looked like a giant high-top sneaker. The mesa started low. Then it sloped upward, flattened off, and dropped straight down. Beyond it was all sky.

She looked out over the trees that covered the mesa. So many tall gray needles. If a careless camper doesn't quite put out his campfire, he could start a huge forest fire, Gabby thought.

Her eyes continued on up to an even higher mesa. This one had no trees and was black. And, although it was July, pockets of snow remained in the shadowed areas of the rock. This made it look grim.

This mesa seemed to say, "I am all-powerful. Don't mess with me." Gabby's eyes followed the outline of the mesa. Finally, her gaze rested on the form next to the mesa.

There it was . . . The Devil's Causeway.

From where Gabby stood, it sure didn't look like much. It was just a small mound when compared to the huge mesas next to it. It looked like someone could skip across it easily.

But Gabby knew differently. She had been there herself many times. The trail wound up through the grassy meadows and tall forests. It went up above the trees. It climbed up a rocky slope to the top where the trail narrowed.

This was where tourists would draw back in awe. For the trail took hikers to the very top of the mountains. They could see forever in every direction.

But just a few yards ahead, challenge and danger awaited those who were unaware. The sides of the trail began to narrow. They narrowed to a point where the walkway was only a few feet across.

On either side, steep cliff walls plunged down to a rocky bottom hundreds of feet below.

Gabby had seen many people climb happily to the top. Then they would see the steep cliffs, grow shaky, and sit down because they were so scared of falling.

Some people would climb over the trail like dogs, clutching rock and pathway with hands and feet. Others would wait and watch in fear as friends and family members crossed the narrow path.

Gabby had seen only one person who didn't seem bothered by the causeway. He was a young man. He did a handstand on the top while his friend snapped a picture.

Although Gabby wasn't afraid to cross, she did respect the causeway. She crawled over it very carefully. Her mother was unaware of the steepness of the trail. Gabby was sure if her mom knew, she wouldn't let Gabby go on her own.

A mosquito bit into Gabby's arm. She flicked it away and continued on her journey. Little clusters of columbines shot out through the grassy slopes. A chipmunk hopped from one rock to another. He paused and looked at Gabby with his right eye.

Gabby greeted the small animal. "*Hola*, little one. How are you this fine day?"

The chipmunk hopped onto three more rocks. Then he disappeared into the underbrush.

COURAGE ON THE CAUSEWAY

Soon Gabby came to what she called the White Wasteland. Trees lay dead all around her. Years ago, beetles had gnawed through these trees, killing them.

The trees had since turned silver and fallen all over the mountainside. Sharp, stubby branches stuck out from every direction. They looked like giant toothpicks scattered on the ground.

The forest rangers have been working hard this year, thought Gabby. The trail was clear for two feet on both sides of her. Then it abruptly became a maze of scattered, dead trees.

Up ahead, she heard voices. It was always fun to meet people on the trail. Almost everyone she'd ever met on the trail was friendly.

Gabby turned the bend. Through the trees she could make out the figures of two people. They were small ones about her size. Great! It's some other kids, she thought.

Gabby came to a crest in the trail, bordered by trees. She stopped. Her body froze. She sucked in her breath. No, thought Gabby. No, no, no!

3

Brush with the Enemy

Gabby couldn't believe what she was seeing!
There in front of her was Jennifer. She and a little boy
were kneeling down by a small marshy area to the
right of the trail.

Gabby drew in a slow breath. What is *she* doing here? she thought.

She didn't want Jennifer to see her. And she didn't want to see Jennifer.

"Jenny, help me find a flat rock so I can skip it across the water," the boy said. Jennifer didn't move. "C'mon, Jenny, show me how you did that. C'mon," pleaded the boy.

"Just find a rock that's flat," Jennifer replied. She still hadn't moved.

Gabby thought maybe she could back away quietly and get out of sight before they saw her. She took a careful step backward. She was afraid they would hear her if she broke a twig. No sound. Phew!

Gabby took another step backward. Jennifer and the boy kept looking for rocks on the ground. The boy suddenly stood up and whirled around. He looked behind him for a rock.

Gabby froze. The boy studied the ground intently. "Jenny, I can't find any flat rocks."

Suddenly Jennifer whirled around and snapped, "Just look! Look all around. There are millions of . . ." Then Jennifer caught sight of Gabby.

Gabby and Jennifer locked eyes. They stared at each other for 20 seconds. Neither made a sound.

"Oh, hi." The boy broke the silence.

"Hi," Gabby said faintly.

"How are you? My sister and I are skipping rocks. Will you help me find a flat rock?"

"Shut up, Nathan!" Jennifer snapped, glaring at her brother.

"But I want to find a rock," Nathan whined. "Will you help?"

"Nathan, *shut up!*" Jennifer looked scornfully at Gabby.

"No, not today," Gabby replied. She looked down at the trail and walked quickly forward. Gabby had to brush past Jennifer, who was on the edge of the trail.

Jennifer stood firm. She huffed when Gabby brushed her shoulder. Gabby moved past quickly.

A boulder stuck in the trail caught Gabby's toe. She tripped forward, catching herself. Embarrassed, Gabby started to run. She disappeared into the trees on the side of the trail.

4

Trapped in the
White Wasteland

Gabby felt her legs picking up speed as she hiked
deeper into the forest. She wanted to get far, far away
from Jennifer and her brother. She wanted to hide—
but where?

The forest floor in front of her was a maze of trees. Dead trees with sharp, stubby branches bursting from the trunks lay all around. They looked like dead soldiers scattered across a battlefield.

The battlefield became fuzzy. Tears blurred her view. Why, why did Jennifer have to be *here*? Of all places, Gabby thought.

Once again, words from Jennifer and Amanda sprang into her head.

"Why do they call you Gabby?" asked Amanda. She didn't give Gabby a chance to answer. "It can't be because you talk a lot. Because I hardly ever hear you say a word." She and the other girls laughed.

Jennifer continued, "Don't you think a little less hair spray on your bangs would be better? I mean, you've got an ocean wave going above your forehead." Jennifer frowned at Gabby.

"Yeah, maybe we could surf on it," laughed Amanda.

"Wave Woman!" Jennifer cried loudly. Both she and Amanda bent over in laughter. Ever since then, Gabby had been called Wave Woman at school.

Gabby touched her hair. The girls in California had all worn their hair that way—long in the back with bangs curled up and teased in the front. It had taken her a long time to get just the right look.

She'd really wanted to grow her hair out in time for her sister's *quinceanera*. Her sister was turning 15 this year. When a Hispanic girl turned 15, everyone celebrated at a big party.

Her sister's quinceanera was next weekend. They were going to have the party in Craig, since more of their Hispanic friends lived over there. Gabby couldn't wait. It was something to look forward to.

Except now her spirits were dampened because of Jennifer and Amanda. Just remembering how they had teased her made her less excited.

But even though the girls teased her, she would never cut her hair. It was long and dark brown, almost black. She liked the way it blew in the wind.

The things she would have liked to change were her nose and lips. Her nose was too short for her face, she thought. And her lips were too full.

Sometimes she'd look in the mirror in the evenings. She'd pinch her upper lip so it would be thinner. It would stay that way for a while. But in the morning, it would always pouf out again.

After the girls started calling her names, Gabby had decided not to tease her hair and spray it up. But now it looked flat and not very pretty. The other way was better. But it hadn't seemed to matter anyway. The girls kept calling her Wave Woman.

A tree leaning on another tree creaked in the slight July breeze. Gabby kicked a stone in the pathway. This was *her* resting place. This was her real home. This was where she could get away from the taunts and jeers and insults of the other kids. The chipmunks and the birds never treated her that way.

Jennifer has no right to be here, Gabby thought. She picked up a stone and threw it into the trees.

"*Wave Woman! Wave Woman! Wave Woman!*" kept screaming in her head. Tears pushed their way into her eyes.

"I won't cry," Gabby told herself. As if warned, the tears stopped. Gabby knew it wouldn't take much for the tears to return, though.

She heard voices behind her. Oh, no, she thought. Are Jennifer and her brother following me? She didn't want to see them again.

Gabby looked around frantically. Where could she hide? Everywhere she looked, she saw piles and piles of dead trees. Gabby spotted a worn path leading deeper into the trees. She decided to follow it.

The broken, dead branches jabbed her soft skin. "Ouch!" Gabby cried, as she walked along the path.

Her right calf scraped against the jagged knives. Poke. Jab. Slice. "Ohhhh!"

Blood oozed out of a fresh cut just below her knee. There were so many short, stiff branches. She couldn't avoid them. They were fingers with long, sharp nails reaching out to scrape her.

She was now deep in the thicket. Gabby drew in a breath. She continued on deeper into the woods. She wanted to get as far away from the main trail as possible.

Jab! Slice! She lifted her left leg over a log. Scrape. "Owwww!"

Gabby looked down to see a white fork mark running from the side of her knee to just above her ankle. The white lines quickly turned red with blood. She kept going. She went deeper into the thicket.

Finally Gabby stopped and looked around. She was trapped—trapped in a maze of needles. Tears of anger and frustration came. She found a smooth patch of log and sat down. The broken branches were just wide enough for her to wedge herself in between.

Gabby thought about her friends from Los Angeles— Griscelda and Rosa. They were so wonderful. They'd shared so many laughs.

Even so, it hadn't always been fun. She and her friends had argued from time to time. But Gabby could never stay mad at anyone for very long. So the fights never lasted long.

Now, Gabby longed to be with Griscelda and Rosa again. She wanted to do the things they had always done.

Gabby remembered going to the mall with her friends. They had shopped and laughed and shared secrets. She craved the delicious Mexican tamales they bought from little food wagons.

Gabby missed having someone to talk to about boys and family and school. Her own quinceanera wouldn't be the same without Griscelda and Rosa there to share it.

The memory of her old friends made Gabby's tears return. Gabby wanted to scream at the mountains. But she held her sobs of despair inside. She was afraid Jennifer would hear her.

Instead, Gabby buried her face in her hands and sobbed. Her shoulders shook violently as her grief came flooding out. For the first time since they'd moved here, she cried and released all of her feelings.

Everybody hates me, she thought. She opened her eyes and saw the fresh cuts on her arms and legs. Even the trees hate me. A fresh wave of tears formed. She sobbed again.

Then she heard a rustling sound on the trail. Gabby froze, trying to be silent. She hoped whomever it was had not heard her. She didn't want to face anyone.

Some hikers must have gone up to the causeway and were now heading back down the trail, Gabby thought.

"Did you hear that?" asked the woman. "Something is moving in those trees."

"Ooh, is it a bear?" asked the man. Gabby could tell by the sound of his voice that he was joking.

"I'm serious. It's something bigger than a chipmunk or a rabbit. It could be a bear."

Gabby remained very still. Just move along, she thought. Please, just leave me alone.

"Should I follow it and see?" asked the man.

"No! If it is a bear, I don't want you to be its lunch."

Gabby rolled her eyes. Tourists, she thought. They all think bears eat people. Gabby knew better.

The voices continued. Only this time, they were getting farther away. The people had passed. Gabby could relax again.

5

A Cry for Help

Gabby sat on the side of the mountain. She rested in between the stubby branches of the dead trees for a long time. After a while, she grew tired of sitting. She looked at her wounds. They were still bleeding slightly.

She pulled out some dried yarrow from her backpack. Yarrow grew in the mountains. Her grandfather had shown her how to dry it and use it to help wounds stop bleeding. She rubbed some on her wounds.

She decided to continue hiking. But what if I see Jennifer and her brother again? Gabby thought. It made her mad that Jennifer could ruin her day.

She'd had a good summer up until now. Then she had seen Amanda at the grocery store and bumped into Jennifer on her favorite trail. All in one day!

They're probably going to The Devil's Causeway, Gabby decided. I'll go up to the saddle instead.

The saddle was a pass in the mountain at the base of the causeway. From there, the mountain curved steeply upward. It was a short, but very steep, hike up to the causeway.

To get to the saddle, she'd still have to follow the same trail as Jennifer for most of the way. She hoped Jennifer had already gone ahead. Then there would be a lot of distance between them.

Gabby planned to turn right at the saddle. There was no trail there, so she wouldn't run into any tourists. And Jennifer would have to go left to get to The Devil's Causeway.

Gabby carefully climbed out of the White Wasteland. She went much slower this time. She tried to avoid the sharp branches. Her wounds had stopped bleeding, but they still stung.

In minutes, she was back on the trail. She hiked along until she came to a mountainside of rocks. The trail cut through the rocks. The rocks were gray with lime green and dusty orange lichen.

Up ahead, she could see the entire trail. It cut across the rocky mountainside. Then it curved upward, starting long switchbacks. The switchbacks cut zigzag paths up the mountainside.

Gabby could see people walking on the switchbacks. She squinted her eyes. She could make out the figures of Jennifer and her brother climbing the switchbacks. Gabby knew that she would be visible to them as well. She hesitated—she didn't want Jennifer to see her.

But that thought just made her angry. "I'm not going to let Jennifer decide where I'm going," she spoke out loud.

Besides, there was only one trail. So she had little choice. Once they got up to the saddle, Jennifer and her brother would go left, and Gabby would go right. Then Jennifer would no longer be able to see her. That made Gabby feel better.

Gabby entered the switchbacks. Old gray trees rose up out of the ground. They stood boldly alone.

The trees had been through it all—storms, showers, blizzards. And yet they remained standing. Gabby wished she were that strong.

The sun blazed down on her neck. The sky was swimming pool blue except for a few tufts of white clouds. Walking up the switchbacks, Gabby began to sweat. She wished the sun would crawl behind a large cloud and give her some shade.

She could see the saddle clearly at the end of the switchbacks. Several hikers were walking back down the mountain. It was around noon—time for lunch. Gabby was hungry. But she decided to wait and eat when she got to the saddle.

Now Gabby could also see the steep trail that curved left. Jennifer and her brother were slowly climbing up the trail. Gabby was glad to see that they were following her plan.

Gabby glanced at the sky. It was still blue. But Gabby knew that thunderstorms often rolled in during the early afternoon. One time, she'd been up on top of the causeway when a storm had formed right in front of her.

She continued to plod up toward the saddle. She passed the umbrella-shaped biscuit root. Her grandfather had told her that Indians dug up the root, dried it, and used it to make flour. Once, her grandfather had made his own flour and used it to make biscuits.

Gabby passed a patch of pretty blue-tipped owl clover. She knew that this clover only grew at higher elevations.

Up ahead, Gabby noticed a tall white bistort plant. On one hiking trip, her grandfather cut open a root of the plant. He showed her the rings inside. The rings told how old the plant was. Once, they found a root with 20 rings. That meant the plant was 20 years old!

Her breathing was getting quicker and quicker now. She had to stop and rest. Gabby looked up. Only one more switchback before hitting the saddle, she thought.

Gabby watched a woman try to go down a steep section of the trail. She slid on the dirt and pebbles, falling on her bottom. "Owwww," the woman cried. Gabby tried not to laugh.

Finally, Gabby reached the top of the saddle. The view was amazing! She decided to rest here and eat her remaining snack. She pulled out her peach and nuts while studying the scene in front of her.

Gabby could see the green valleys reaching out below. Clusters of tall trees looked like carpeting on the valley floor.

She grabbed her water bottle from its holder and drank two big gulps of water. It was always so refreshing after she'd been walking.

Gabby felt better. The scabs on her legs were throbbing slightly. But she felt like she'd gotten her second wind.

Gabby looked around. It was so still up on the saddle. She could see forever. There was no sound anywhere—not even a bird or grass waving in the wind. Gabby enjoyed the peace and quiet for a moment.

Her heart sank as she looked out at the view. Dark clouds were off in the distance. That meant that she wouldn't be able to get off the trail before the rain. She didn't have rain gear with her. And being on top of a ridgeline in a lightning storm was very dangerous.

She decided to turn around and head back. It had taken her an hour and a half to climb to the saddle. But she knew it would only take about 45 minutes to go back because it was all downhill.

Gabby turned to head back down. All of the other people were making their way down the switchbacks. They were headed toward the rocky trail at the bottom of the mountain. They must have seen the storm coming in too.

Gabby had walked down one leg of a switchback when she heard something. It was faint. She paused. There it was again.

It was not the sound of a hawk—or branches breaking—or the wind. It sounded like a voice. She listened and heard it again.

Yes, it was a voice. She couldn't tell if it was the voice of a man or woman. But she was sure it was a voice. Gabby held her breath and listened carefully.

There it was again. She couldn't tell where the voice was coming from. It seemed to be behind and over her. She looked around, but she didn't see anyone.

The voice came again—this time from above. She looked up, but again she couldn't see anyone. However, Gabby was now sure that the voice had come from the top of the causeway!

6

To the Rescue?!

Gabby paused for a moment to form a plan. There were two ways to reach the causeway.

She could run back up the switchback to the saddle. The switchback was flatter and would be easier to climb. But it was also the longer way.

The top of the causeway was at least 50 yards straight up from the saddle. Fortunately, the forest rangers had built log steps up to the causeway.

Or she could scramble up the side of the mountain. The mountainside was much steeper. But it was the shortest way to reach the steps.

"Help!"

For the first time, Gabby understood the words being yelled. She glanced back at the switchback. It will take too long, she decided. I'd better go up the mountain.

Gabby began climbing up the mountainside. She used her hands, knees, and feet as support. For the first time, she realized she must have left her walking stick back in the White Wasteland. It would have helped her now.

She grabbed the stunted branch of an Englemann spruce tree and pulled her body up. A continual spruce bush blocked the path in front of her. It covered the steep ground with its prickly green. She had no choice but to climb over it.

The branches dug into her calves, sending sharp reminders of her wounds from the dead trees. Fresh blood oozed out of her skin. With every step, the branches tangled around her calves and ankles. The stiff branches scraped off her raw skin.

Gabby moved slowly over the spruce patches. She felt like a turtle. Every second she was on the mountainside, the storm drew closer.

Gabby wondered if she'd made a mistake. Maybe she should have taken the switchback. Even though it was farther, she wouldn't have been stalled in this tangle of spruce.

Gabby glanced all around. She looked for another hiker who could help. There wasn't one person on the switchbacks or the saddle. Two stragglers were marching on the path by the stone mountainside.

Gabby screamed loudly, "Help! Help!" But the hikers continued on. They hadn't heard her.

Gabby tried to ignore the pain as she continued climbing. The steepness of the mountainside also caused problems for her. She struggled to climb straight up the side of the mountain. Gravity worked against her.

She thrust her leg into an open area between the shrubs. Her legs pounded with pain. Her foot slipped, and she fell down into a patch of spruce.

"Ooof!" Branches sliced across her arms and cheek. She paused for a moment to catch her breath.

"Help us! Please, help us!" The cry came from above.

"Com—coming," Gabby let out in short, quick breaths. She scrambled up again. She wanted to scream from the pain.

She forced herself to keep climbing. Three, maybe four, more strides and she'd be at the steps.

She carefully placed her right foot in front of her. Sure of her footing, she stepped down. Gabby shifted her weight. She found an empty spot and stepped down again. She repeated these movements steadily. Finally, she was at the steps.

There were no spruce shrubs to deal with there. But the steepness of the steps caused Gabby's tired legs to shake.

She kept climbing—once again using hands, elbows, knees, and feet. Her fingers gripped logs and rocks to pull herself up. She was gasping for breath. But she didn't slow down.

"Come quickly!" cried the person from above.

"I'm c—coming," Gabby gasped. This way up the mountain was hard enough just walking. But this scrambling was exhausting.

On top, she caught her breath and looked around for the person who was yelling. Nathan stood about 20 yards in front of her. He was pointing at the causeway. Gabby scrambled along the path to the boy.

"Look! She's stuck!" he yelled.

Gabby peered at the causeway. Jennifer was huddled

on the narrow path. There was nothing but sky and two feet of rock on either side of her. Jennifer's eyes were wide with fear.

Seeing Jennifer reminded Gabby of all the cruel things she'd said to her. *"You mean you can't even read! I can't believe it!"*

"It looks like something my grandmother would wear!"

"Wave Woman! Wave Woman!"

"You need to get her off," Nathan told Gabby.

Gabby walked over to the edge of the causeway.

"Gabby, you have to help me," Jennifer pleaded. "I can't get back. I can't get off this . . . *thing!*"

For a moment, Gabby couldn't get the thoughts of Jennifer's harsh words out of her head. *"You mean you can't even read . . . can't even read . . . can't even read . . ."*

"Gabby!" Jennifer said from the causeway.

"Wave Woman . . . Wave Woman . . . Wave Woman . . ." The words washed over Gabby again and again.

"GABBY!" Jennifer screamed. "Why are you just standing there? Help me off!"

"Why'd you go out there?" Gabby asked calmly.

"I thought I could do it. And I did. Then I looked over the edge. It's so steep. I can't make it back. I just can't. If I move, I'll fall. I just know it."

Gabby couldn't help thinking of all the hateful things Jennifer had done to her. Why should I help *her*? Gabby thought.

As if Jennifer knew what she was thinking, she pleaded again, "Gabby, please."

7

No Way Out

Why should I help her? Gabby immediately felt guilty at her thoughts. A cold breeze swept over her. She looked up at the sky. The dark gray clouds were getting closer.

In the near distance, Gabby could see the bottom of a cloud. It was dropping in wispy fingers. The rain was coming. Thunder grumbled softly.

"You have to save my sister," said Nathan.

Gabby turned to him. He was so young. Did she dare send him back down the mountain by himself? She had no other choice.

"Do you remember the way you came up?" Gabby asked Nathan. He nodded.

"There's only one trail. I need you to run down that trail and get someone to help us. Can you do that?" Nathan nodded again. He turned and started running down the trail.

"Just stay on the trail!" Gabby yelled after him.

She turned and looked at the narrow, rocky path. The trail leading up to it was made of finely crushed rock and dirt. But the rocks grew larger at the causeway.

The narrow ledge was uneven. Rocks were stacked on top of one another. Bright orange lichen covered the gray rocks. It was the color of Halloween candy.

The trail curved in an S form. Jennifer sat at the farther end of the S.

Except for a bird chirping on a ledge, the only sound was the slight howl of the wind. Sometimes there was a low grumble of thunder. The air was cool and made the bumps on Gabby's legs stand up.

Gabby looked at Jennifer's huddled body. What could she do? She knew she couldn't carry Jennifer off the causeway.

Perhaps there was another way off the ledge. Gabby looked around her. She searched for another escape.

A grassy slope rose gradually behind Jennifer. It was no more than 20 yards wide by 40 yards long. But to get to it, Jennifer would have to continue on the narrow ledge for several feet. Then the trail continued around the China Wall from there.

The China Wall was a huge ribbon of rock. It wrapped around the valley like a fortress. Snow hid in its shadowy pockets.

If Jennifer went that way, it would take her twice as long to get back to the beginning of the trail. And she'd still have to get off the narrow ledge.

To her left, Gabby could clearly see the lake. It stretched out in the shape of a shark.

Gabby looked down over the edge of the causeway. She saw the basalt rock and boulders about 500 feet down. They looked like pebbles from this distance.

There were conifer trees next to the rocks. The small trees looked like they'd been planted a few years ago for a Christmas tree farm.

As she looked around her, Gabby realized that there was no other way off the causeway. She had to get Jennifer to come back the same way she had gone out. But how?

As Gabby studied the causeway, she realized something was wrong. Something was different. Every other time she'd come here, she'd been calm. She'd been able to pick out a path across the ledge.

But today it was different. She felt something strange deep inside of her. She couldn't shake it.

Then it dawned on her. She was scared—really scared. She, Gabriella Soliz, who had climbed over the causeway many times, was frozen in fear. It was as if Jennifer's panic had gripped them both.

A bee buzzed around Gabby. Tiny flies gathered on her arms and legs as she studied the situation. She brushed the flies from her wounds.

There's no way to help Jennifer off, she thought. It's hopeless.

Gabby heard an airplane streaming above the clouds. But she couldn't see it. It was amazing how clear the sound was coming from such a distance. It sounded like the plane was a few feet from her.

Gabby glanced up at Jennifer. Jennifer was quiet now. She looked into Gabby's eyes. Gabby saw something she hadn't seen before in Jennifer's eyes— hopelessness. Jennifer had given up.

8

Rain, Wind, and Fear

Black clouds stretched their thick arms out and surrounded them. In a way, Gabby thought, it was comforting. The clouds cut off their view of the dangers that lay below.

All of a sudden, they were in another world. There was no up or down or sideways in this world—just the path before them. It was like a dream.

Gabby shook her head. No! she thought. It's not a dream! The steep canyon walls *are* real. And Jennifer *is* trapped out there.

Suddenly, lightning cracked into the side of the China Wall.

"Gabby, HEEEEEELP!" Jennifer screamed. Even Gabby was startled by the strike. The clouds spit out rain. The cold droplets jolted her skin. It seemed that even the weather was against them.

Okay, Gabby, think, she told herself. What could she do? Her mind raced. Nothing—it was hopeless.

No, it can't be hopeless, she thought. Both sides were battling it out in Gabby's brain.

"Gabriella, my love, you are a strong girl. Be strong," she heard her grandfather say in his soothing Spanish. *"If you ever get into trouble in these mountains, the first thing to remember is to stay calm. Then you will think of an answer. You can do anything you set your mind to. Remember, stay calm."*

"Stay calm! How can I stay calm?" she asked out loud as if her grandfather were there. Another lightning bolt flashed. The raindrops fell heavier.

"Be strong, Gabriella . . . you can do anything . . . be strong . . . you can do anything . . ."

She looked out at her classmate. Jennifer's hair was plastered against her face. She was crying quietly now. Her arms were wrapped around her legs, and she rocked back and forth. I will have to cross the causeway to Jennifer, Gabby thought.

Gabby's legs didn't want to go. Her heart didn't want to go. I can't do this, she thought.

"Be strong, Gabriella . . . Be strong . . ."

Gabby bent down on the wet earth. Pain shot up through her body. Her leg wounds cracked from the pressure of her bent knees. But she didn't let this stop her.

Gabby thrust her hand forward. The rocks were wet and warm from baking in the sun all morning. The soft lichen on the rocks eased the blow to her hands.

She immediately thrust her right knee forward. The pebbles poked into her skin. Her left hand moved forward. Then she moved her left knee. She had moved her body one length forward.

"Good, Gabby. Keep it up. You're doing great," she told herself out loud. "Focus on the path in front of you."

The rain came down cold and hard now. Gabby felt her body shivering. She couldn't believe that just a little bit ago, she'd been sweating. Now she longed for the sun to return.

Gabby once again picked up her right hand and set it down one pace in front of her. Again she lifted her right knee, then left hand, left knee . . . She shifted her weight forward. She focused again. Right hand, right knee, left hand, left . . .

A deep gash in the ledge drew Gabby's eyes toward it. The gash acted as a lens. Gabby could see the steep canyon wall and the ribbon of rock miles below.

You're gonna die. You're gonna die. You're gonna die, raced through her head. Gabby froze. Her breath came in short, quick spurts. She sat back on her heels.

A pool of turquoise blue caught Gabby's eyes. Off in the distance, the pool of melted snow glowed in the gray-green rocks. Small mounds of white snow surrounded one edge of the pool. From where Gabby sat, the blue water was the size of a child's backyard pool.

Gabby looked back at the trail. She realized that if she started sliding on the rocks, she could slide right off to her death.

I have to get off here, she thought. She reached her left leg backward to move back off the causeway.

"Don't *leave* me up here!" Jennifer pleaded. "Please, don't leave me here."

Gabby looked at Jennifer. She saw terror in Jennifer's eyes. "Please, Gabby, please," she pleaded.

"*You are a strong girl. Be strong . . . be strong . . . be strong . . .*"

Gabby pushed away her negative thoughts. She tried to focus on the big picture. I must keep going, thought Gabby. Once again, she began the slow process of crawling on the narrow ledge.

All of a sudden, it hit Gabby—what will I do when I get out to her? She hadn't thought that through. If she went all the way to Jennifer, Jennifer might grab her. Then they'd both fall to their deaths.

If she only went part of the way to Jennifer, what good would that do? Gabby was angry that she hadn't thought of this earlier.

I need a plan, Gabby thought. What will I do when I get out to her?

Gabby looked at Jennifer. Jennifer was afraid because she thought she was going to fall. Why did she think she was going to fall?

Why hadn't Jennifer worried about falling on other parts of the trail? Gabby focused hard. She tried to imagine Jennifer crawling over the rocks.

It wasn't working. She could only imagine herself going over the rocks. How had she done it? When the clouds had surrounded them, she'd felt safe. Why?

When she went over the rocks and focused on the trail, she wasn't worried. But as soon as she saw out of both sides of her eyes, she became afraid. Then she could see that the trail was only four feet wide and the drop meant certain death.

"That's it," she said out loud. "It's our sight that causes the fear. I have to get Jennifer to focus her eyes on the trail, not the surrounding dangers."

But Gabby knew that just telling Jennifer to focus would not be enough. Somehow she had to make her focus. She had to cut out her vision on both sides. That's it! she thought. Gabby then knew what she would do.

Gabby continued climbing on the trail. Fear struck her again for a moment. But then her grandfather's words returned.

"You can do anything you set your mind to."

Her grandfather's words gave her strength. "You're right, Grandfather. Okay, Gabriella, just concentrate," she told herself. "Focus on the rocks in front of you. And whatever you do, don't look down!"

9

Focus on the Plan

Rain and wind hammered in from the west. The rain washed the dirt from the rocks. A dusty smell filled the air.

Looking forward, Gabby guessed that she had moved only a couple of feet. She still had about 12 more feet to go.

One thing at a time, Gabby reminded herself. First things first. She had to focus.

She eyed a bluish green stone only three feet in front of her. She focused on that one stone. She lifted up her right hand and right leg and placed them squarely down in front of her. The wet rocks cut into the skin on her knee.

"Blue rock. Keep your eye on the blue rock," she repeated to herself. Next she lifted her left hand and left leg and placed them down about a foot in front of her. She shifted her weight forward. She came closer to her focus rock.

The storm continued to pelt her. Thunder cracked and roared around her. But Gabby kept moving.

Gabby stopped when she was about three feet away from Jennifer. "Don't reach out to me," Gabby said.

"What?" Jennifer replied, looking confused.

"Don't reach out to me when I get to you," Gabby repeated. She spoke louder this time. "I want you to do something. I'm going to make something, and I want you to watch me."

"Gabby, just get me off this thing!" Jennifer screamed.

"Jennifer, stop!" Gabby looked firmly at Jennifer. Jennifer looked at Gabby and quieted down.

"Now, I'm going to make something that will help you. But you must do exactly what I say. Can you do that?" Gabby's voice was firm.

Jennifer nodded.

Gabby dug in her pockets and pulled out two orange gloves. They were the gloves she wore to work in their garden at home. "Give me your sunglasses," said Gabby.

"My sunglasses?"

"Yes, give me your sunglasses." This time Gabby said it more firmly.

Jennifer handed Gabby her sunglasses. Gabby pressed her thumbs on the right lens. She pressed hard and out it popped. She did the same thing to the other lens.

Gabby took the glasses and put them on her face. Then she took a glove and folded it until it was firm. She slid the glove between her left temple and the arm of the glasses. She took the other glove and repeated the process on the right side of her head.

When Gabby looked down at the ledge, all she saw was the trail. The air around the trail, as well as the view down the canyon walls, had disappeared behind the blinders.

Gabby pulled out the gloves first. Then she took off the glasses. She handed them both to Jennifer.

"I want you to do what I just did," Gabby told Jennifer.

Jennifer took the glasses and gloves. She repeated Gabby's actions. When Jennifer was finished, she looked at Gabby.

"Look at the trail," Gabby instructed Jennifer.

Jennifer looked down at the trail.

"Is that better?"

Jennifer nodded.

"Now, I want you to focus on the trail. Try to find an object—a stone or something—to focus on. Keep your eyes on that. Just keep looking down. We're going to crawl out of here together. Do you understand?" Gabby asked.

Jennifer nodded.

Thunder cracked and lightning lit up the sky around them. Both girls looked at each other. They knew that this was their only chance.

Gabby carefully placed her hands on the trail behind her. She swiveled her feet slowly around so that she was facing the opposite direction. Gabby started to slowly crawl back off the ledge. She didn't turn around to see if Jennifer was following her.

Soon she heard movements behind her. She relaxed a little. At least Jennifer was following her!

Together they made the slow journey along the ledge. The thunder cracked and split around them. Gabby's legs wanted to go more quickly, but she knew she had to be slow and steady for Jennifer's sake.

Once, Gabby glanced back at Jennifer. The blinders were doing their job. Jennifer was focusing on the trail and crawling forward slowly.

Icy droplets of rain dug into their skin. But they kept moving.

"Noooooo!" Jennifer screamed suddenly.

"What! What?" Gabby swung her head around just in time to see one of the gloves slipping from the glasses. It fell silently over the edge. Both girls watched it fall to the rocks below.

"Oh, nooooooo! HELP! I'm gonna *die*. I'm gonna *die*. I'm gonna *die*!" Jennifer's eyes were darting back and forth rapidly from one side of the causeway to the other. Her body was shaking.

Gabby swiveled around in the causeway. If she didn't calm Jennifer down now, she would go over the edge.

"JENNIFER!" Gabby screamed.

Jennifer now had her eyes shut tightly. Her head was shaking back and forth. Tears flowed out of her eyes. She was saying, "I'm gonna die. I'm gonna die. I'm gonna die . . ."

"JENNIFER, STOP IT!" Gabby screamed. "STOP IT! STOP IT! STOP IT!"

Jennifer stopped and looked at Gabby.

"Now you *are* going to come off this ledge. And you're going to do it *now*! Bring your right knee toward me."

Jennifer hesitated.

"DO IT NOW!"

Jennifer moved her right knee forward. She started to look down.

"Don't look down!" Gabby said firmly. "Keep your eyes on my hands. Now move your left knee forward."

Jennifer obeyed.

"Now your right hand."

Gabby crawled backward on the trail. As Jennifer came forward, Gabby backed up. They continued this way until Jennifer came to a bend in the pathway.

"Now, there's a little curve in the path. We're going to go left a bit," Gabby explained.

Jennifer glanced down at the bend. She started to shake again.

"LOOK AT ME!" Gabby commanded. Jennifer's head snapped back up to look at Gabby.

"Now, you're going to bring your left leg forward and to the left a bit," Gabby explained. Jennifer moved.

"Now follow that with your left arm, and shift your weight over when you feel solid ground." Jennifer moved again. Slowly, she shifted her weight.

"Good!" Gabby said. "Now bring your other leg and arm to meet them."

Jennifer did as she was told.

"Okay, we're almost there. Bring your left leg toward me," guided Gabby.

Lightning once again lit up the sky around them. But they didn't notice. Gabby kept coaxing Jennifer forward.

Finally they made it to the point where the path widened. "We made it!" Gabby told Jennifer.

The girls hugged tightly. Jennifer sobbed heavily into Gabby's shoulder. Gabby breathed a deep sigh of relief.

10

A Good Different

Dread washed over Gabby as she walked to school. This was the first day of the new school year.

Back in Los Angeles, the first day of school had been exciting. It meant seeing all of her friends again. They had compared new clothes and talked about how different the boys looked.

But here Gabby walked alone. And no friends would be waiting to share summer stories.

She looked ahead. The big brick building looked like a prison. Kids were hanging around outside, laughing and talking.

No one noticed Gabby as she walked inside the school. She passed the other students silently and headed straight to her locker. No one greeted her. No one ran up to her and screamed her name like she heard other kids doing. No one even noticed she was there. She felt invisible.

Gabby opened her empty locker. She stared, lost in thought.

"Hey! How was your summer?" She turned and looked. It was Josh. He had the locker next to hers.

He looked different. What was it? He was smiling at her. Something seemed different about his smile. That's it! she realized. There were no braces.

Josh's face glowed with a summer tan. Gabby also noticed that he had grown. In fact, Gabby concluded, he looked kind of cute.

"Fine. And yours?" Gabby said.

"Awwwwesome!" He leaned on his locker door as if looking at her for the first time. "You've changed. Did you get your hair cut or something? You look different."

Gabby felt funny as he stared at her. She looked down at her shoes.

"No," she muttered.

"Well, something's different." The bell rang and Josh was off. He turned around and yelled back. "But it's a good different!" He smiled broadly and ran off.

Gabby couldn't help feeling a little excited as she walked to class. Although Josh wasn't the most popular boy in school, kids liked him because he was so much fun to be around. Maybe they could be friends . . .

Gabby's thoughts were interrupted as she walked into her homeroom. The feeling of dread returned. Most of the kids were sitting in their seats talking to one another. Their eyes would dart from the door to their friends as they checked out each person entering the classroom.

Gabby spotted Amanda. Her hair was longer and blonder than last year. It curled under perfectly at the ends. She was wearing a brand-new sweater and jeans. Her lightly tanned skin looked perfect against the peach color of the sweater. She was leaning toward Jennifer, whose back was to Gabby.

For the first time, however, Gabby saw Amanda and Jennifer in a whole different way. Last year, she had thought that Amanda and Jennifer were perfect. She believed they never had any problems or fears.

But Gabby had been wrong. This summer had shown her a whole new side of Jennifer. Jennifer wasn't strong and perfect all of the time. Sometimes she was afraid and needed help—just like everyone else.

Gabby gazed at Jennifer and Amanda talking so seriously. She wondered what Amanda's weaknesses were.

Amanda glanced toward the door and saw Gabby. Gabby could see her lips form into *Wave Woman*. Gabby stood firmly and stared back at Amanda. Last year she would have slunk off to an empty seat. But this year, she didn't care what Amanda called her. Gabby was ready to stand up for herself.

Jennifer turned slowly to look at Gabby. Gabby walked to her seat before making eye contact with Jennifer. She didn't care what Jennifer thought anymore either.

Gabby still felt lonely. But she didn't feel powerless anymore. She had her strengths and her weaknesses, just like everyone else. This gave her self-confidence.

The teacher walked into the room just as the second bell rang. "Good morning, eighth graders. I'm Mr. Brannon, your homeroom teacher. The first thing we do every morning is take roll."

Mr. Brannon started calling off names.

"This is so lame," a red-haired girl on Gabby's left said. She leaned over her desk and smiled at Gabby.

"What?" asked Gabby.

"This roll call business. It's so lame."

"Yeah," Gabby agreed.

"I'm Heather. I was in your math class last year. I remember when you moved here. I have a hard time with math. But the day you started school here, I got an A on a test. I figured you were my good-luck charm."

Heather, who had thousands of freckles on her face, continued to smile at Gabby. "So I hope you have math with me again this year." She smiled even more broadly.

Gabby smiled back.

"Gabriella Soliz," Mr. Brannon called.

"Here," responded Gabby.

The rest of the period was spent going over schedules and rules. By break time, Gabby was ready to stretch. She also wanted to talk to Mr. Brannon.

She walked up to the teacher's desk and waited while other students asked their questions. Finally he was looking at her. "My name is Gabriella, but you can call me Gabby."

Mr. Brannon looked at her. "But Gabriella is such a beautiful name. Are you sure you want to be called something else?"

Gabby hadn't thought about it before. Everyone, except her grandfather, had always called her Gabby. He's right, she thought. I've always loved Gabriella.

"Okay, Gabriella it is." She smiled at him and walked to the restroom.

Most of the girls had cleared out by the time she got there. She looked at her face in the mirror. She *had* changed since last year. Her face was thinner and her eyes looked larger.

She hadn't noticed the changes at home. But coming back to this familiar bathroom, Gabriella had expected to see the same person in the mirror. Somehow, though, she looked different.

Jennifer suddenly came out of a stall. Their eyes met.

Seconds later, Amanda burst through a stall door. "Why, if it isn't Wave Woman."

Gabriella glared at Amanda. Then she looked at Jennifer. Jennifer looked embarrassed. She put her head down, refusing to meet Gabriella's eyes.

"So Wave Woman, did you ride any waves this summer?" Amanda laughed and studied herself in the mirror.

Gabriella looked at Amanda. "Couldn't you do better than that, Amanda?"

"What?" Amanda swung her head around.

"Couldn't you come up with something more original? Come on. I thought you were more clever than that," Gabriella said in a slightly shaky voice. Then she turned on her heels and walked out of the restroom.

Gabriella felt such strength—such power! Okay, so her voice had shaken a bit. But she'd done it. She'd just stood up to Amanda Bart, the most popular girl in school!

Why hadn't she done that last year? It wasn't so hard. Why had she worried so much about what Amanda and Jennifer thought of her? What a waste, she thought.

At lunchtime, everyone headed to the cafeteria. By the time Gabriella got there, the line stretched around the lunchroom. As she went to stand in line, she noticed she would be right behind Jennifer and Amanda.

Last year, Gabriella would have stopped and waited for others to go in front of her. But this year, she walked up and leaned against the wall directly behind the girls.

Amanda turned around. "Ooooh, if it isn't Wave Woman!"

"Shut up, Mandy!" The words were surprising. Even more shocking was who they came from. Jennifer was glaring at her friend.

"What?!" Amanda stared at Jennifer.

"I said, 'Shut up!' " Jennifer repeated.

"What's gotten into you?" Amanda asked. "All morning you've been moping around." She paused and then said slowly, "You know I don't *have* to be your friend."

"What? Is that how you see it? Like you're doing *me* a favor?" Jennifer asked her friend. "I can't believe it."

Jennifer rolled her eyes and walked around Amanda. She stood in front of Gabriella. "I have something for you."

Gabriella looked at Jennifer. What could she possibly have for me? Gabriella wondered.

"What? What are you doing, Jenny? What do you have for *her*?" Amanda barked.

Jennifer turned and looked at Amanda. "I think it's time for you to find someone else to grace your presence with."

Amanda's jaw dropped, and she slumped against the wall. Jennifer turned back to face Gabriella.

Jennifer reached into her pocket. She pulled out something orange. It was the glove—the one that hadn't fallen. "I haven't forgotten," Jennifer said.

Gabriella looked at the glove. A flood of memories came rushing back. She remembered the fear on Jennifer's face, the storm that had pelted them, and the steep canyon walls.

"Here, you take it," Jennifer said. She thrust it out to Gabriella.

"No, you keep it. You earned it," Gabriella said, smiling at Jennifer. Jennifer smiled back and turned to wait in line with Gabriella.

Yes, thought Gabriella, this year would be different.